Whistling Wings

By Laura Goering
Illustrated by Laura Jacques

"I see it!" cried Marcel. Down below he could just make out the long necks and black beaks of the swans who had already arrived.

"Get ready!" called his father. The "V" of the flock separated into smaller groups. Marcel followed his parents toward an open patch of water. They skidded forward, then plopped backwards onto the lake. Marcel plunged his beak into the water and drank.

"Time to rest," said his mother. But Marcel was already sound asleep.

Marcel loved his new home. He feasted on wild celery and sago pondweed. He played with the other young swans. Best of all, he didn't have to fly anywhere.

But every day the trees lost more leaves. Every morning the ice crept inward from the shore. The air was filled with the whistling of wings, as swan families set off to the south.

One frosty November morning, Marcel's father announced, "Time to go!"

"Go?" asked Marcel. "Why can't we stay here?"

"We have to leave before the lake freezes over," said his mother. "It's a swan's way of surviving the winter."

"We leave first thing tomorrow," said his father.

That night Marcel dreamed of flying. He flapped his wings, but made no headway. "Are we almost there?" he asked his father in the dream. But the answer was always the same: "A thousand miles to go. Keep flapping!"

M arcel woke up exhausted. *No way*, he thought. *I can't fly all that way*. And he waddled into the rushes to hide.

The morning stillness was broken by the sound of squawking swans, soft at first, then building to a tremendous noise. Marcel put his head under his wing to shut out the racket. He stayed there all day, occasionally lifting his head to listen. When it was quiet, he crept back to the lake.

Everything was still. His plan had worked—the flock had left without him . . .

So why did he feel sick? He looked up. *Maybe I can catch up with a few stragglers*, he thought. But the sky was as empty and gray as the lake. Marcel slid into a tiny patch of open water and started to cry.

A furry head popped up in the water next to him. "What's eating you?"

"I got left behind," said Marcel. "How will I survive the winter?"

"Do it the muskrat way." The head vanished into the inky water.

"What's that?" cried Marcel. "Wait! Come back!"

"Hey, do you want to learn or not?" The muskrat's head reappeared closer to shore.

Marcel crossed the ice to investigate.

"First, chew a hole in the ice. Cover it with plants and mud to make a roof, like so. Push plants up through the hole every day so it won't freeze completely, and you've got a nice feeding station, see? But get busy—soon the ice will be too thick."

"Thanks," said Marcel, "but I can't swim underwater."

"Suit yourself," said the muskrat, and he disappeared under the ice.

Suddenly, there was a great whooshing sound and everything grew dark for a second.

"Need food? This way!" screeched a bald eagle overhead. "Hop to—I'm not waiting!"

Marcel took to the air just as the eagle disappeared over the treetops. "I'm coming!" he cried.

The eagle rocketed to the river, then arced upward with a flopping fish in his talons.

"Mississippi Lock and Dam #4. Fine dining, open year round," said the eagle. "Enjoy!"

"It's too deep!" objected Marcel. "And I don't eat fish!" But the eagle had already vanished into the clouds.

Marcel circled back to the lake. The sky was growing dark and his patch of water was crusted over with ice. One more cold night and there would be no food until spring.

Marcel put his head under his wing and closed his eyes.

"Hey! That's no way to sleep!" came a voice from the shore. "C'mon! I've got the perfect bed for you!"

Marcel hesitated, then waddled over to the shore.

"Here," said the raccoon from next to a hollow log. "This end is mine, but that one's free. Climb in, think warm thoughts, and before you know it—weeks have gone by!" The raccoon climbed into the log, curled up in a ball and fell asleep instantly.

Marcel tried going in headfirst, but he ended up with his neck inside and his body outside. Then he tried to squeeze his bottom in and almost got stuck.

Finally, too tired to go back to the lake, he hollowed out a trench by the log and lay down with a sigh.

The clouds had lifted and the full moon cast spooky shadows across the ice. Marcel closed his eyes and tried to remember what it was like to be warm and full.

When he first heard the whistling sound, Marcel thought it was a dream. But a familiar *hoo-hoo-hooing* made him sit up with a start.

Two ghostly figures were circling the lake.

Marcel knew those voices. "Mom! Dad!" he cried. "Over here!" He stumbled over the log, onto the ice, and into his mother's embrace.

We thought you were with us," she said. "Thank goodness you're safe!"

"We turned back as soon as we realized," said his father, hugging them both. "Now let's get you something to eat!"

The three of them broke a hole through the thin ice. They took turns scouring the bottom for the last bits of sago pondweed.

"Okay," said his father. "Let's go!"

"Now?" asked Marcel.

"Sure," said his mother. "Look at this glorious moonlight!"

His father took to the air, with Marcel and his mother close behind. Higher and higher they rose, until the lake below faded into darkness.

"How far is it, Dad?" Marcel asked.

"A thousand miles," answered his father.

Marcel settled into an easy rhythm. His stomach was full and he felt warm despite the frigid November air. With his father in the lead and his mother beside him, a thousand miles didn't seem so far after all.

Keep flapping, he told himself. *Just keep flapping.*

For Creative Minds

Tundra Swan Fun Facts

Tundra swans are birds. Birds are the only animals that have feathers. Like mammals, they breathe air and are warm-blooded. Birds hatch from eggs.

They are also called Whistling Swans because their wings "whistle" as they fly. They have a high-pitched call that can be heard at great distances.

Adult tundra swans are between 3 and 4 feet with a wingspan of 7 feet. Adult tundra swans weigh between 13 and 20 pounds (males are heavier). *How tall are you and how much do you weigh?*

When angry or scared, a tundra swan will hiss and raise its wings. With the wings spread open, the swan looks very big and that helps to scare off other animals. The wings have a hard bony spur on the elbow of the wing, especially large on an adult male that could hurt other animals.

Their webbed feet help them swim.

Tundra Swan Life Cycle Sequencing Activity

See if you can put the swans' life-cycle events in order to spell the scrambled word.

Cygnets stay with their families about a year and get adult plumage at about 15 months. They will mate and start their own family when they are four or five years old.

The female lays three to five cream colored eggs that are about five inches long in each nest.

The babies, called cygnets, have gray, down feathers and pink on their beaks that gradually turns black. They leave the nest and can swim within 24 hours of hatching.

The female incubates the eggs while the male stands guard. The parent birds can't protect eggs from large predators (wolves, polar bears, or humans) so they will often fly away from the nest making it harder for the nest to be found.

Eggs hatch after 31 or 32 days—usually in late June.

The young cygnets eat plants, worms and other invertebrates to gain strength. As they get older, they tend to eat more plants and seeds, like their parents.

The male and female work together to build a large, open bowl-like nest in tundra ridges close to a pond or lake. They use grass and moss to build a nest that is about one to two feet across and about 12 to 18 inches deep.

Migration Fun Facts

Migration is the survival movement of animals for breeding or to follow food or water during changing seasons.

Migrating animals may travel short distances (up and down mountains) or very long distances, like the tundra swans.

Migrating animals will follow the same route year after year. Because of that, scientists can predict when and where you can go to see migrating animals.

Many animals migrate in the fall to avoid cold winter weather and then back again in the spring. Other animals only migrate a few times in their lives, like a female sea turtle returning to the area she was born to lay her eggs, or salmon swimming upstream to lay their eggs.

Swans migrate south from the breeding grounds in September or October and will travel in family groups or small flocks.

Tundra swans will stop at lakes and ponds in the northern US and Great Lake areas to rest and eat. Then they will take off again and fly over 1,000 miles without stopping.

Tundra swans start to arrive in their wintering grounds at coastal estuaries, lakes, and ponds in mid-November. Then they turn around and migrate back to the tundra from their wintering grounds in mid-March.

During the summer, tundra swans nest in the northern tundra above the Arctic circle. Each pair claims their territory and guards it carefully. They'll return to the same area year after year.

Animal Adaptation Matching Activity

All animals have physical or behavioral adaptations that help them survive in their environment and with seasonal changes in that environment. Physical adaptations are parts of their bodies that help them move, make their homes, and get their food. Some animals have learned behavior adaptations to help them survive: like migration or hibernation. See if you can match the animal adaptations that are listed below to the right animal. *Can you tell which adaptations are physical or behavioral?*

1.

- These birds fly thousands of miles to warmer weather.
- Like many birds, they have huge wings to help them fly long distances. Their bones are hollow (less weight) for flying.
- They usually eat plants but will also eat some small animals (insects or small clams, etc.).

2.

- These mammals' long back feet have hair between the toes that they use to help paddle through the water. They use their long, flat tails to steer, like a boat rudder.
- They build "pushups" or piles of plants in the ice where they store food to eat and where they breathe during the winter.
- Like tundra swans, they are mostly plant eaters but will eat small animals if they are really hungry.

3.

- These birds of prey have large, sharp talons (claws) to catch and hold onto their animal dinner.
- They soar high in the sky on air currents and use their good eyesight to see prey below. Depending on where they live, some of these birds migrate ahead of freezing ice; others do not migrate at all.

4.

- These mammals are true scavengers and will eat whatever they can find: plant or animal. Their long front paws have five "claw fingers" that they can use to open things—like trash cans!
- They don't hibernate but they do sleep snug in their dens for long periods of time in the winter. On warm days, they'll stretch and grab some food.

a. Eagles

b. Raccoons

c. Tundra Swans

d. Muskrats

Answer: 1. c, 2. d, 3. a, 4. b

To Molly—LG

To Fred who has been "the wind beneath my wings"
for such a long time. With all my love—LJ

Thanks to Roland J. Limpert of Maryland's Department of Natural
Resources and co-author of Tundra Swan (Cygnus columbianus),
The Birds of North America for verifying the accuracy
of the information in this book.

Publisher's Cataloging-In-Pblication Data

Goering, Laura.
Whistling wings / by Laura Goering ; illustrated by Laura Jacques.

p. : col. ill. ; cm.

Summary: Marcel, a young tundra swan, tires halfway through the winter migration and
stays behind while his parents and the flock continue south. He asks for advice from other
animals about how to survive the winter, but their ways are not right for the swan. "For
Creative Minds" section includes fun facts about tundra swans, migration, and an animal
adaptation matching activity.

Interest age level: 005-009.
Interest grade level: K-4.
ISBN: 978-1-934359-12-9 (hardcover)
ISBN: 978-1-934359-30-3 (pbk.)

1. Tundra swan--Juvenile fiction. 2. Birds--Migration--Juvenile fiction.
3. Birds--Adaptation--Juvenile fiction. 4. Tundra animals--Adaptation--Juvenile fiction.
5. Swans--Fiction. 6. Birds--Migration--Fiction. 7. Tundra animals--Fiction.
I. Jacques, Laura. II. Title.

PZ10.3.G64 Whi 2008
[E]   2008920386

Printed in China

Sylvan Dell Publishing
976 Houston Northcutt Blvd., Suite 3
Mt. Pleasant, SC 29464